August 2016

To John and Samia,

All the very best!

Emma

The Blue Box

Emma Abdullah

ISBN:
ISBN-13:

To the children of Syria. In memory of all the candles that were blown out too soon and for all the children and everything they could have been.

“ It all looks really nice but there is one thing wrong: the children are not smiling. They are sad because the only thing they have left besides their hope is each other and they are too scared to face the world on their own. What scares me the most is that I can’t find Nour anymore and this time, I know it’s not hide and seek.”

-Cover illustration by Rima Shaaban, age 10
(Deirezor, Syria)

CONTENTS

ACKNOWLEDGMENTS

With far more appreciation than I can put into words, I'd like to thank everyone who supported me in the making of this book. I cannot express enough thanks to Ingrid Maclean and Stephen Glover for all the help they have been; it would not have been possible without them. Thanks to Audrey Christie and my uncle Nabeel for being the first people to believe in me and a huge thank you to my big family and my friends for all their support and encouragement every step of the way. Thank you also to Mr Tareq Rajab for the support of the New English School and to the SAMS (Syrian American Medical Society) for all their work in trying to make the world a better place. Finally, my heartfelt thanks to my parents and to Ryan, who kept me going every time I wanted to give up and who believed in me at times more than I believed in myself.

PREFACE

Roses for my Mum

These roses I pick with joy and with glee,
All the beautiful ones just for my mummy
Because I love it when I see her smile
And then I know it's all worthwhile.

Oh this one is nice, just like her eyes,
It will wipe up her tears when she cries,
And this one, I know, she'll keep next to her,
She'll treasure it always and forever.

And when she feels lost, feels all alone,
When her heart feels cold, feels like a stone,
She'll look at my rose, feel happy again and
she'll keep smiling because it's never the end

So here's my bouquet, my beautiful flowers,

Though I might have to wait a couple of hours.

We're only visiting her tonight,

Oh how I wish I could hold her tight.

When I see her, I always smile, it's true.

I'll say, "Here are some roses just for you."

Then hold back my tears and try to be brave

As I place my bouquet onto her grave.

I wrote this poem when I was twelve; it was one of the first poems I had ever written. I'd learnt at school that poems rhymed and so after counting syllables, rhyming lines and reading it through several times, my poem was finished. I hadn't thought of what I would do with it then, just finishing it seemed enough. I hadn't written it for anything or anyone in particular, so there was nobody to give it to either. My first poem just sat there, bored and without a purpose.

I thought that if I wasn't going to do anything with it, I might as well put it somewhere, just in case I ever wanted to look at it again, so I found a purposeless empty box that probably felt as unneeded as my poem and placed my very first poem inside it.

It was a dark blue box with nothing on it but a few scratches, an indication that it had once served a purpose. My box looked nostalgic and wistful. It seemed to yearn for another life, another world, now so far away. I took out a marker and smiled at my box. *'IN CASE I EVER NEED THIS'* I wrote in red on its side before placing it on my shelf. It stayed there for a year.

The next time I used my box was in July of the following year when I wrote one of my first short stories. After spending a few minutes contemplating what to do with it, I remembered my first poem in its blue box and decided that the story could go in there too.

I took to writing short stories every so often after that. It became a hobby, an escape. Sometimes I wrote stories so that I could put them in my blue box; I didn't want it to feel alone. I wanted to feed it with my thoughts. I wanted it to live again through my stories so I wrote about ordinary people, imperfect people who lived average lives shaped by circumstances. I wrote about normal people who did everyday things. My stories were sad sometimes but they were real. I imagined that was what my box would want. A real story. A story it could relate to. I imagined my box wouldn't mind pain because it was true. My box would understand that lives are unfair and that the good people don't always win. That was how it started. It started with a box on a shelf and stories that were for no one in particular.

In March 2011, the Syrian civil war started. I didn't understand the politics behind it. To me, it was a conflict like any other. I imagined that soon things would go back to normal. They didn't. The war dragged on. Thousands of children were tortured and killed. Human rights were violated. I lost some friends. I have never heard again from some others.

I wanted to do something. I didn't want to be a spectator. I would not be a spectator. But what can a child do? What can one child do to save another? What does a child do when nobody else seems to be doing anything? Is there something a child can do when nobody seems to care?

My thoughts kept drifting back to the question. I told myself I did not have the power to do anything. I had to leave it to someone else, to someone older, someone more influential, someone with the power. And yet. Yet it did not seem right. It did not seem right to do nothing at all. It did not make me any better than those who committed crimes if I stayed silent about them.

It was then that I saw it: a dark blue box with nothing on it but a few scratches and capital letters in red, 'In case I ever need this'. I took my box down from its shelf and pulled out the first sheet of paper. My poem. I read it silently. Over and over again I read the poem of a child burying a mother. Suddenly it was relevant. Suddenly it had a purpose. Suddenly it meant something; it meant so much more than it had five years before. I rummaged through my blue box and found more poems and stories. They spoke to me in words they never had before and, at that moment, I knew I had found my weapon.

So here it is, here is my attempt at making a difference. Here are the stories I have written, some when I was young and others several years later. Here is a little part of me going out into the world, hoping it will give a voice to those who do not have one of their own. Our words are our only weapon in this fight; it would be a shame to not at least try.

To everyone who will never get a chance to tell their story and in memory of the children of Syria, I want to be able to say I tried.

1

Blue Box Story Number 1, March 2013

Call of the Jasmine

This story is in the form of a letter by a little boy called Karim who tells a story not many people have wanted to listen to. His story is around us though, but maybe we've conveniently not been able to see.

Dear Santa,

I hope this letter finds you well. I'm not very good with posting letters because baba used to mail them for us. I don't know exactly where to send it either because this is the first letter I ever write to you. I didn't know about you before; Joe told me yesterday. He says you're a man in red who makes good children happy and who brings them presents. I never got a present though. I don't understand because I've always been good.

Maybe it's because you couldn't find my house? But Joe says your reindeer always know where the good children are. Maybe you forgot me then. That's okay, I understand, people have forgotten us so many times.

If this letter reaches you though, please try to remember me. My name is Karim and I live in the basement of the little house that used to be a bakery. It doesn't make bread anymore so you can't follow the smell but I know, if you look really hard you'll find us. The bakery is destroyed because destruction makes people go away so, if you hide inside destruction, you're safe. It's what baba says but to me the bakery is just scary and I miss my home.

Dear Santa, if this letter finds you, please pay us a visit. I don't have cookies to offer like Joe says I should but I promise mama will make you feel welcome. She always does with the crying children.

I know where I live is not very pretty and I know there's not much in it for you but mama says we're beautiful where it counts.

Santa, I don't want any toys but could you please bring some smiles with you and some tissues for the tears? It scares me to see mama cry, could you bring nights that aren't so cold? Santa, please, could I ask for some colour and for the streets not to be so grey? Tell the men in uniform that they'll get presents too if they put down their guns.

At night it frightens me to sleep next to Aziz because he shuffles around all the time and I know he's much older than I am and he's not allowed to cry, but when they told him he'd never walk again, I hid my face to let him sob. He says I'm not allowed to write to you because you're not for us but Joe says Santa is for all the children. If so, then please, could you bring a new leg for Aziz and bring Fridays without screams? Please tell the giants that jump at night to let us sleep in peace.

Santa let me know how Reema is because I haven't heard from her for so long. I need to tell her I still have her doll but, no matter how hard I knock at her door, there's no answer anymore. It scares me because I know Reema can't live without her doll.

I know I'm being a selfish boy for asking you so much but it would make me smile to see the jasmine grow again where the children used to play.

If this letter does find you, could you please bring me a dog? When I see the rescue shows on TV, they're always saving animals. Would they save me if I were an animal?

I know it's not December and it's too early for letters to Santa Claus but I thought that maybe, if I wrote early enough, you'd make the time for me or maybe it's just that somewhere, a part of me is scared I won't be here anymore by December.

Please don't forget me, Santa. It makes me happy to think that somewhere out there, somebody cares.

Love,

Karim

"I dream of giving birth to a child who
will ask, Mother, what was war?"
Eve Merriam

2

Blue Box Story Number 2 , April 2012

Mashed Potatoes

I find it funny how different people define happy moments. I mean, what is a happy moment? How do you define happiness? To me, happiness is the end of suffering but that is a difficult thing to comprehend for those who do not suffer as I do. Suffering is when every heart beat is more painful than the preceding one and when every breath seems to be a waste of death.

It is as if I can see every second painfully passing by, as if each one stings me before letting the next take its place. It is now that I realise how painfully long a minute is; how far it stretches before slowly drowning into the next and ever so slowly dissolving into infinity, mocking you all the while. I am numb. I think I have forgotten how to feel. Should I be happy? Afraid? My feelings are wolves, each fighting for the biggest part of me and tearing me apart. My emotions are in such a tight knot inside my stomach that it is complicated to determine whether fear, anxiety or pain claims the greatest share of me, or perhaps the greatest share of what is left of me.

Today my guest will come for me. I do not know his name nor what he resembles but I wait for him. I wait for my guest like a child on Christmas Eve. I wait, locked up in this room. If I could run, would I? Would I fight if I had the chance? What is there to fight for? I wouldn't have it any other way.

A knock on my door. I sit up. He has come.

"Your special meal," says a voice, sliding a shiny metal tray through a flap in the door. It is not him. I had forgotten about my meal. I get up from the hard bed on which I was resting and take little steps in order not to fall because of the chains on my feet. I sit down on the cold concrete floor and place the tray over my lap.

Why are my hands shaking? I order them to stop but they refuse to obey me.

I don't think I'm hungry. Today is my special day; I could have had anything at all to eat. I could have had anything I wanted to but I chose mashed potatoes. Not that there's anything wrong with mashed potatoes. Mashed potatoes will be my last meal. The fork feels cold in my hand as I take small bites. I can vaguely remember a toy I had as a child; it was a small colourful clown with exaggerated features and a wide grin. When I pressed its nose, it would start singing and telling me to clap my hands if I was happy and I knew it. I think I am happy.

How do you judge a man? We all seem to be very good judges of other people. So, how is it that you do it? Do you judge him by the good things he does? Or do you just ignore that and focus on the sins? Who are we to judge? In this prison cell, sits a murderer. This murderer is me and I would not change a thing, not a chapter in my story. What I did, I did it because it was my duty. They say revenge is a confession of pain. In my case, it was a confession of hatred and sorrow and disgust and grief and so many other things for which words don't exist. Here's another thing that doesn't exist: humanity.

My son was the most precious thing I had. He was the only thing I had. Harry was only three but I sometimes felt he could understand me like nobody else. He was a part of me. You can't just rip parts out of people like that. You can't. You can't crop out a piece of the soul, just like that. You're not allowed.

The day I lost him, the day they extracted a piece from me, I swore I would find the person responsible and make them pay the bitter price. The authorities took care of it for me; they found the man and he was sentenced to prison. Then they let him out. They let him out for good conduct. Good conduct? Is that what a life is worth? Is that really your definition of what a life is worth? We're such funny people.

There is no word for the loss of a child. It is a piercing pain that brings you to your knees, screaming and crying and begging. If this man's death could compensate for a millionth of the sorrow I felt, then I would have to kill him.

So I did it. I killed a man with a cold heart, feeling absolutely no pity. He was easy to track down. I screamed. I cursed. I cried. I shot. The next day the police were at my house. I didn't try to hide.

They say I had no right, that I may not create my own justice. To me this *is* justice and I have no regrets. I would do it again and again and again. Tears are streaming down my cheeks and my eyes are bright red. My hands won't stop shaking. My soul aches and aches and aches. Why won't he come? Let him come and finish me. Let him finish me. Let me join Harry in heaven, away from this world of mad people and crazy ways. I wish my heart could be squeezed until it beats no longer. I wish my lungs could be beaten and blocked so that no air may enter this repulsive body. Today is my happy day. Today the pain ends.

A knock on the door. I sit up. He has come.

The door opens and a tall man tells me to follow him. I get up, taking one last look at the mashed potatoes - Harry's last meal. I follow, without a word, into a room with white walls where I am ordered to lie down on a pale bed with bars to which I am attached tightly. I find myself smiling. A man whose face I cannot see rubs my arm with alcohol. Why disinfect it? It's ironic really. Why do you disinfect criminals' skins before injecting lethal poison into them? Because it's ethical? Humane? Yes, of course.
Tonight, from six to seven, there will be no lights in the prison cells. Instead, there will be darkness mixed with a deafening silence because all the prisoners will know what it means: that another one of them has been executed.
A syringe is prepared. I close my eyes. I think of Harry. I think of my clown and its grin. I

wish I could see my guest's face. I wish I could clap my hands.

"Any last words?" he says. I can only see his eyes.
"Yes," I reply softly, "Thank you for freeing me."

"The strictest law sometimes becomes
the severest injustice."
Benjamin Franklin

3

Blue Box Story Number 3, June 2012

Born to Kill

He couldn't have been any more than fourteen years old. Innocence and confusion burned in his eyes as he stood there, not knowing what had happened to him. I looked at his face and, suddenly, I saw myself. It was like staring into a mirror of the past: it was me a few years ago, before I became a monster, before I was afraid to stare at my own reflection without hating myself.

I will always remember that day: the day they came for me and changed my life forever. I was only a child and I knew not of all the world's atrocities until I, myself, became a part of them. They came into my house early in the morning, screaming. They destroyed everything. I remember being woken up by the noise and running downstairs to check what was going on. There were men dressed in black with guns in their hands, holding my mother. Tears streamed down my bright cheeks and I screamed. I screamed because my mother was crying and my father was on the floor and I did not understand. My mother begged them not to hurt me; she said they could have anything they wanted. But they wanted me. I didn't understand or, perhaps, I refused to understand; I was only a child, I wasn't an object! What did they want from me? They left me no time to realise. Two men grabbed my shoulders, despite my frantic kicking and protesting and the pleas of my desperate mother.

From under the table, I spotted two teary eyes intently staring at me: those of my little brother. Somewhere in my confusion, I felt relieved that they had not seen him, that he would not have to suffer my same fate. I couldn't help noticing a little red ball that he was agitating as if to tell me something. It was then that it hit me. We had argued over who should have it the night before and I had been told off by my mother for not being a more responsible and protective older brother and letting him have the little ball. I remember giving in and laughing as I saw that he had slept with his prize to make sure it was not taken away.

His confused little eyes stared into mine. Amidst the tears, just for a split second, I forced a smile as if to tell him it would be alright but somewhere, in our innocence and ignorance, we both knew. I died a little inside as I watched him place the ball near his heart. One man put his hand over my mouth to muffle the screams, so that nobody would hear the pleas of an innocent child. I heard a gunshot and a shriek. They took me away.

I never saw my mother again. In fact, I never saw anyone I knew ever again. All I saw every day was the other side of this world - the ugly side that not many people know about. We were twenty-two children. Twenty-two children who hadn't smiled for years; twenty-two children who had become adults too soon.

R.S. handed me a gun on my first day. R.S. was the leader but no one really knew why he was called that.

"'When I tell you to shoot, you shoot", he told me, "you kill or you get killed. The choice is yours."

I didn't know what was happening to me, I didn't know what I was doing, or why. I always hoped I would wake up in the loving arms of my mother and she would comfort me, telling me it had all been just a nightmare. But I never woke up. This nightmare became my reality. I became the nightmare. At first I cried all the time: the long walks with so much weight on my skeletal back killed me and the short cold nights with the floor as my bed made me ache in the morning. I soon learnt that frail tears would not save me. In fact, nothing can save us from this unpredictable world in which we are all adrift.

We were treated like objects, beaten, burnt and thrown around. The rebels who dared to utter a word were made to pay the price and served as a warning for the rest of us. There was nobody to trust; some were made to kill their own families and in the end I began to wonder if I could trust even myself and the demon growing inside me. We weren't given food or water; we had to find our own when we could. The other children didn't speak; their bodies were present, but not their souls. They did as they were told and it was as if the beatings no longer hurt them.

Soon I became one of them myself. I remember the first time I had to pull the trigger. It was a young boy about my brother's age: the little brother I had loved and was no longer there to protect; the little brother who would have been so ashamed of me. He hadn't done anything, he hadn't hurt anyone but he was a victim all the same. He was outside playing. I had cried and said I couldn't do it. My trembling fingers had said they didn't have the strength. My eyes had stung so much but they had forced me. It was either me or him. If I didn't kill him, I would be killed so I had to choose my life over his. He deserved life more than I did.

I despised myself from that day on; I hated all of it. This pointless war that we children were forced to fight for reasons we could not comprehend. The fact that it didn't matter if you were innocent, it didn't matter how old you were because war was war. The biggest battle I fought was with myself because I hated the person they had made me. And for whom? For what? What was the point of a war that made children orphans, that left mothers crying? Is it really all there is to this world? How does suffering help things get better? Does a life mean so little? Is that what we are all destined to become as we get older? In my naivety, I had promised myself that, once I was old enough, I would put an end to it; that I would speak out and make the world a better place.

The years passed by. I grew. I became older, tougher and harder to hurt. My heart was cold; I had no mercy; I was a machine. Not all of us made it though, some didn't survive. They fell down one day and nobody picked them up. We

walked on, it was just another lost life; we had seen it before.
R.S. handed him a gun. "You kill or you get killed," he told the young boy, "The choice is yours."

“You can no more win a war than you
can win an earthquake.”
Jeannette Rankin

4

Blue Box Story Number Four, October 2012

Different Shoes

I stared back undeviatingly at the person looking at me but refused to make eye contact – people like me did not make eye contact. I tried to focus on a different part of him – his socks. I stared intently at his bright red socks and then looked up and flashed him a bold, out-of-place grin. Our eyes mistakenly met and without thinking, I burst into fits of shrieks and began rocking myself back and forth. It was perfect. I turned away from the mirror and threw myself onto my bed, rethinking everything I was about to do, rethinking the whole show I was going to put on for the sake of proving something to myself. It was going to be quite an act indeed.

The building was a dark brick-red that seemed to have been freshly painted. Backpack on my shoulders, I advanced towards it but kept my gaze focused on my shoes. It would only be three months. Three months in this new school before summer came along, bringing the movers' van with it and we would be off to a new place.

Classroom D13. "You must be Austin," said a tall lady with silky dark hair wrapped up in a bun on her head. She had square glasses at the tip of her nose and although I could tell that she was not very young , she had made great effort in concealing even the slightest wrinkle on her face. I avoided eye contact. She had shiny black heels and skin-coloured tights. "You must be Austin?" she repeated. I started flapping my arms.

"Excuse me?" I twirled them in circles. She gave me a hesitant look but motioned me inside. "This is our new student, Austin."

I stared back at all the eyes that scanned me from top to bottom. There were a few smiles. For a second, I reconsidered everything. Perhaps it would be better for me to say a casual hello, run my hand through my hair and give one of my winning smiles. It would be better, easier. But I had enough of being successful, being good-looking, being the son of so and so. I had to prove this to myself, I had to know how it felt. I took a deep breath, focused on a spot on the floor and covered my ears before letting out a long, deafening shriek.

The class was taken aback. I shut my eyes and kept my hands on my ears, I could feel my face growing warmer. Was this really what I wanted? Yes.

"Austin, are you alright?" she looked concerned. I could hear a few sniggers from one of the back rows. Why were they laughing? Did they find it funny? Were they enjoying the show? I uncovered my ears. "Austin," I whispered and directed myself to a seat at the back.

***

"A-U-T-I-S-M," he whispered, "It's called Autism."

"Can he understand people?" asked another boy.

"No," answered Logan, "he doesn't understand anything, he's stupid, all he does is scream. He shouldn't even be here." They laughed. The days ever since I had started here had all been very similar. I would sit alone on my bench. There would very often be a group of people around me, trying to see what I would do if they provoked me. I gave them what they wanted: I screamed so loud someone would have to break them up and calm me down. Everybody was intrigued yet amused; I scared some of them. People fear what is different. I got very much into my act, I felt like it was a part of me, I no longer had to think of my next move, it all came spontaneously.

Autism. Autism. He's autistic. Yes. No. He doesn't understand. Something with his brain. It's a disease. He's handicapped. I know him.

He had flashy sneakers, the new Nike ones. His socks were white.
"If it isn't Autistic Austin!" he smirked, "Done your screaming for the day?" There was a bit of mud on his left shoe.
"Look at me when I'm talking to you, hey!" I was tired. I wasn't up to it. "Hey Austin!" he said shoving me into the girl behind me. I screamed. It made him laugh. The punch on the face that followed didn't, though. He lay on the floor as a teacher pulled me away. I grinned – this time, not out of place.

I'm not sure what I was expecting, I guess I had too much faith in the world. Perhaps I hoped to feel like I was normal; I thought they would try. Pity? I got that. I got hate too, but there was never anyone strong enough to give me a chance, anyone strong enough to forgive me for being different. I got a few smiles but never anything more. What was I expecting anyway? I wonder how many people out there are willing to stand from the crowd and speak their mind. How many of us out there would stick up for someone because we felt it was right?

There's something about those who are different that disturbs us. We don't like them because they scare us, because they're something new. Our insecurities build walls around us because we're all adrift in this unpredictable world. I learned more in those three months than years of education could ever have taught me. There is no Richter scale to measure pain; it leaves you vulnerable. It's not pain you can get used to, not sorrow that you can tame. It leaves you broken, broken but alive. Although many do claim to be tolerant, I never felt at ease or in my place. In fact, not even adults managed to treat me somewhat normally. The sorrow of not being accepted is one that is deeply felt. I realised how nasty people are, how selfish. I do catch myself feeling uneasy, even now. We live in a world where some people have already lost the game before having begun and there were times when I came home crying, not for me but for Autistic Austin and for all the others out there, who are different.

“Being different is a revolving door in your life where secure people enter and insecure exit.”
Shannon L. Alder

5

Blue Box Story Number 5, November 2012

Mind your Mind

He advances towards me and I know from the look in his eyes that this time I'm in for it. I can feel the fury burning inside me. This time, I will not let him hurt me. He moves swiftly, jumping from bed to bed and even hanging in mid-air at times. I try to imitate his movements but end up on the floor. My head is throbbing and every part of my body aches; it feels like I've been shot.

I scream.

I should have known it was a trap.

Two men enter the room and I am certain they want to take me away but I can't fight back. Pain shoots through my veins as a needle is poked somewhere into my shoulder. Slowly, the aching subsides and I have this eccentric feeling, somewhat like floating on a cloud. It feels unusually good. Everything subsequently goes dark but I close my eyes anyway. The darkness will protect me.

My eyes open again, only to realise that I am still in the same room. There is a bothersome feeling in my left arm and when I try to rub it with my hand, I cannot: I am strapped down to my bed. The walls are the same memorable pale white colour and only very faint light is glimmering through the window. I now realise that they have caught me, that I will be spending the next few days here, in this same position. I already know from experience what it will be like. However, I also know that it is inevitably pointless to try to free myself: they are many, and I am one. There are millions of them whereas I am defying the world by myself.

Sometimes I forget.

I forget that I am never by myself. They are always watching over me. I believe I'm alone but I never really am. My name is Dmitri and I live in a dark closet invisible to the rest of the world; nobody knows, nobody understands. It's all in my head, it's my reality. My name is Olga too, and Steven and Vladimir and Faye; we are so many, embodied in just one. It is tiresome, confusing, but it is a necessity. We face the world together. We have schizophrenia.

He enters the room with his white coat and stern look. Apart from the nurses who feed me, he is the only visit I have had in a week. He looks at my ridiculous face and notes things down. If I was not stuck in this straitjacket with my hands tied behind my back, I think I would punch him - maybe even kill him before he kills me, and kill all the other staff while I'm at it.

What am I thinking?

Stop it Olga

I know it's you, don't tell me things like that... I really would want to kill him though. I know that when he smiles at me it's because he's secretly plotting to do it first and my being stuck here defencelessly is the hinge of his plan.

Olga! Stop! I don't want to kill anyone, please!

Yes, I do, I want to kill all of them.

I can't bring myself to decide which is worse: my delusions or the moments of sanity where I actually realise who I am and what I'm doing. It troubles me because I try, I truly do, but they're trapped within me now and I just can't fight them.

I know I need them.

No I don't.

Vladimir you know I don't need you.

I know they're my only friends because nobody else is there for me. I hate them. But I need them.

Life hasn't always been this way. I was something before this chaos; I was someone. You have to be prepared to fall if you're going to rise. I guess I just wasn't. I was successful; I was bright, my family was well-off. They all believed that I had a future ahead of me. My mother was a bit uneasy with the idea of my going abroad to pursue my studies but I assured her that I would take care, and that I would be alright.

I really thought I would, I thought I had all the chances on my side to be great. Then life struck me, like a strong punch in the stomach, knocking you down and I never got back up. It was like everything around me had shattered, like a glass bottle shattering into millions of pieces as it touches the floor. Everything that had once comforted me and made me feel safe was gone. My secure warm home, away from all the dangers of the world, was no longer there for me and I felt exposed and vulnerable. I realised I had always been protected - by my parents, by our situation and that there were so many things out there I had never experienced. So I sought refuge in the unreal, in the delirious. I tried to hide behind the walls of insanity and I went mad, all by myself, in a world I had not known before, with only my mind as my best friend, yet greatest foe.

"Dmitri, we've talked about this before," he says in a grave voice. "You can live an almost normal life; you can limit the delirious episodes. You must continue your medication."

The medication helps me see things clearly. It helps limit the hallucinations and increases the periods when I am lucid, the periods when I am well. I am not going to take it because it will hurt me which is exactly what he wants. I take the white pill from his hand and place it under my tongue.

Don't swallow it!

I won't, Steven.

I sip the water and put the glass back down. It's what I have been doing for fifteen days. When he turns around, I carefully spit it out. He'll never hurt me.

"We're going to let you see your mother," he says. The door opens and I see a frail lady come in, accompanied by the men in white. I can see that her hair is becoming white at the root – everything is becoming strangely white - and that she has lost a lot of weight. I imagine the misery I have put my family through, how I have torn them apart.

She comes closer to my bed and brings a shaking hand close to mine. Her tired milky blue eyes fill up with tears.

"Dmitri," she whispers, "I love you."

Suddenly, I know from the look in her eyes what she wants. I can feel the fury burning inside me.

"Olga!" I scream, "Olga, get away!" I begin to kick and agitate my fists.

"I hate you!" I holler, "I swear I'll kill you!"

I try to grab her so that I can strangle her but the men in white reach her first and usher her out of the room.

Pain shoots through my veins as a needle is poked somewhere into my shoulder. Slowly, the aching subsides and I have this eccentric feeling, somewhat like floating on a cloud. It feels unusually good. Everything subsequently goes dark but I close my eyes anyway. The darkness will protect me.

My fierce Olga will remind me of the sweet, so sweet, desire to kill.

My witty Steven will warn me against the notorious white-coated man and his poisonous pills.

My always-devoted Vladimir will need me, as I will need him.

They will all protect Dmitri.

I will protect Dmitri.

I will protect Dmitri.

Schizophrenia will protect Dmitri.

“If you think this Universe is bad, you should see some of the others.”
Philip K Dick

6

Blue Box Story Number 6, September 2012

Behind the Door

I press my ear against the wall and hold my breath. I can no longer hear them. I try to listen harder.

I hear footsteps—I think they're his. I count the number of steps he takes; I suppose he has reached the door. Then I hear it swinging open and I know almost for sure that he is leaving. I rush to the window to make sure. I get a good look at him - he is wearing a black suit with a red tie and holding a briefcase in his left hand. He casually glances at his watch and walks a little faster towards his BMW, which matches his suit perfectly, and takes off without looking behind.

I pace the room; my mind feels numb from all the thinking. Then I hear it – a loud cry. I retreat to my place against the wall. I can hear them sobbing and saying things but I cannot make out the words. There is the sound of a baby crying too; I assume it's Mona only because I think I recognize her cry. I have become used to the distinctive sound of each of their cries. This one is the baby.

He returns at about half past eight. Nine o'clock on Tuesdays. I hear the familiar sound of the BMW tyres on the gravel followed by the headlights as his car pulls in. I take my place and wait. It will begin at about half past nine. Half past ten on Tuesdays.

At around 9 o'clock, the screaming begins. *He is early today*; I imagine he has had a bad day at work. He bellows at them at the top of his voice. I hear the sound of bottles crashing onto the floor and the shriek of six year-old Taylor. There are some cries and some swearing, words that I have never heard before but that the little ones are probably used to. Then, silence.

Silence can mean a lot of things: silence can mean pain, it can mean sorrow, it can mean acceptance or fear. You can let it define you and scream for you, you can let it be your voice and hide behind it. You can surrender to silence and let it guide you, or let it build its walls around you. It is very often in what we cannot hear that there are the most words. Silence is the most powerful weapon.

***

Her backpack is streaked with different shades of blue. It is one of those expensive brand bags that everyone wants; they are an easy way of showing you have money. Her clothes are neat; she wears a long-sleeved shirt and a red skirt that reaches below her ankles. I know they are expensive clothes because I have seen them in a shop before. She looks small and frail in them, like she's been forced to wear them. Taylor is also wearing long sleeves today and a dark blue hoodie that makes him look much older. Their faces seem to lack emotion and there isn't any light in their eyes. Slowly, they get into the BMW. She holds Taylor's hand as if to protect him. Their father sits himself in front of the steering wheel and sympathetically waves at me before closing the door. I don't wave back. I watch them pull out of the driveway, on their way to school. She even tries to force a smile because smiling twelve-year-olds are normal, because going to school is normal, because it's better to be normal.

What does it feel like to live a lie? To wake up in the morning and put on your fake smile of convenience? To keep quiet when people talk because you're afraid you might say something, let the truth slip out just a little bit and then have to lose yourself in an even bigger lie? What does it feel like to be afraid to come home, to live amongst the screams, to watch the people you look up to crumble? What does it feel like to fear the people you love? To love, yet hate them? To want them to die, yet be beside you? What does it feel like when you're hurting everywhere, mentally and physically; when you have nowhere to escape to and everyone thinks you're fine and happy? They don't know – nobody knows. They don't know what happens when the door closes. Nobody knows the story behind the door.

I don't know where they go after school. They come home in their black BMW with their expensive clothes and backpacks. Today, he is wearing a red shirt that matches her skirt. Happy families do that sometimes: they wear the same colours because they are united and content. A father with a decent job, a lovely wife who cooks a nice meal for his return, and their three children – a boy and two girls. The perfect family in their perfect house. They could fool us all if they wanted to.

She gets out of the car, still clutching Taylor's hand. For a moment, our eyes lock and it's like I can feel every single emotion in her – like she's using her eyes to call for me, to beg for my help. I look away.

Half past nine. He isn't home and it isn't Tuesday. I wonder if he's decided not to come home after all, to go away before he does them any more harm. They would be better off without him. Suddenly, I hear the sound of the tyres on the gravel and my heart sinks a little bit at the thought of the deceptive calm that had come over me. He is back. I rush to the window, hoping to understand the reason for his bizarre late return. I see him get out of the BMW and open the trunk, only to pull out a colourful kids' bicycle and a huge doll. He then pulls out a bouquet of roses and makes his way to the house, closing the wooden door behind him.

I find it difficult to comprehend. Is he sorry? Does he think he can buy their silence? Are they going to be alright after all? Was everything solved and were they going to celebrate? I comfort myself with that last thought, simply because it's always comforting to tell yourself things are going to be alright, because even if part of you senses you're lying, it's comforting to shut it out, shut out reality and pretend, because pretending is nice.

Eleven o'clock. The screaming begins and this time I don't need to take my place at the wall so that I can hear them. It has never been this loud. I feel like barging into their house and screaming at him to stop. I hear the baby, I hear Taylor, I hear their mother. Should I call the police? Am I indirectly responsible? *No, it has nothing to do with me, I should mind my own business.* I force myself not to listen, to pretend I can't hear because pretending is comforting and pretending is nice. The cries are louder. I turn up the television volume and drown out their pleas. Then there is silence.

Seven o'clock in the morning. I am awoken by a somewhat familiar sound but am too sleepy to properly identify it. It takes me a few minutes to realise that it is coming closer and that now, it seems to be right under my house. Curiosity overcomes my desire to go back to sleep and I walk to the window. I see an ambulance followed by two police cars and before I have time to make any assumptions as to what it could be, two men rush out of my neighbour's house with a stretcher, carrying someone whose face I cannot see. I stick my face to the glass, trying to identify the person, in vain. Is one of the children hurt? I only see a black sleeve. The men put the stretcher into the ambulance and drive away, their siren tearing open the warm silk of calmness in the neighbourhood. My heart beats fast – I can try to lie to myself and say it had nothing to do with me but somewhere I know I'll always have ignored that cry for help.

I try to compose myself and rethink the situation. Suddenly I notice something outside in the garden. She is sitting on the grass, staring up at me, wearing shorts that reveal her swollen legs. I have to squint a bit but I am shocked to see the wounds; they are all over her arms too. Calmly, she looks at me as if to ask me to take a look, to look at what I had done to her by ignoring her persevering cries. My heart is pounding inside my ears, *surely it couldn't fully be my fault*, but the look in her eyes is so accusing, it burns. She continues to sit there, alone in the grass, still looking up at me as if to ask me why, and the worst part is I know I'll never be able to answer. Can you be blamed for something you did not do? Can you be blamed for letting silence speak for you? If I were to be judged, would I be guilty for surrendering to it? Did my silence mean acceptance or fear?

All of a sudden, she stands up and she smiles – as if to say it was okay, that sometimes it's better to act like things are alright; pretending is safe. She walks up and caresses the BMW with her hand before entering her home, entering the truth, behind the door.

"If you want to keep a secret, you must
also hide it from yourself."
George Orwell

7

Blue Box Story Number 7, December 2012

Do you Have a Pen?

There was nothing worse than being on call. It ruined the weekend, tampered with your sleeping pattern and had you surviving on high doses of caffeine for at least another two days. It was tiring, tedious and dull but on the other hand, I had missed the family gathering. There was nothing worse than family gatherings: all those conversations of trivial importance, the petty arguments and endless discrete glances at the watch. On the bright side, I had missed that but my heart had sunk a bit upon hearing the disappointment in my father's voice when I had to excuse myself from his birthday celebration. When he had asked if there was any chance I could be replaced for this one time – that I could get the weekend off just this once – I had lied and said no. The truth was, I preferred to spend the night alone in these dim hallways.

Perhaps I am a selfish man but I console myself with the thought that we are all greedy, that in the end it's all down to us and getting through the day. I've learned never to get too attached, never to hang on too tightly because that is when you fall the hardest. But honestly, it is not without guilt that I sat, not without a slight constriction in my chest, that I sat on my neglected white chair, being the terrible selfish man that I was.

Hospital walls rock you into a lying, deceptive calm. They lie. They have a sickly colour that sings you into oblivion, that tells you you'll be alright when you have no chance. I always wondered why they were painted as they were, such a sterile, lying, manipulative white. It was of no solace to the patients. If I were in hospital, I'd want my walls painted bright explosive colours.

I patrolled the corridors, stopping sometimes to read the number on a room although really, I knew them all by heart. How does it feel to be just a number in a room? Just a number amongst the numbers, a bed amongst the beds, a patient, a disease? A disease amidst the diseases.

She stopped me mid-track, rushing over to me with her clipboard and countless papers and a panicked look on her face. She was saying something about patient 102. Patient 102? I had never spent very much time with him. He was an elderly man of little words with rickety health. He was another number – a passing number, a temporary number, like all the others. Sooner or later, they would all leave and, terrible as it was, terrible as it sounds, you got used to it once you'd been here a while.

His heart was beating slower, his breathing more difficult and it was only a matter of hours before they thought they would lose him. With all the composure I could gather, I walked across the corridor to room 102.

His skin was pale, his milky eyes devoid of light, his soul tired. He lay there, listening to the beeping and watching the little waves on the monitor go up, then down, then up, getting flatter every time. I don't know if he noticed – maybe he didn't really realise what they meant.

"My son", his voice came out as a hoarse whisper. "Tell him," he begged.

"I'm sorry sir, I don't..."

"Tell him I'm here." His eyes were watery. "Please, tell him I'm here."

"Sir, your son knows you are in hospital."

"But call him," he pleaded. "Tell him to come, that I'll be leaving. I know I'll be leaving. I have to speak to him."

I wonder what it feels like when you know it's the end of the road, when you know that fighting is futile because sometimes you have to give in to life – It's only fair.

I walked to the sterile white phone and punched in the numbers. I felt a nagging uneasiness, one I could not really account for. Being the bearer of bad news is a terrible thing; sometimes you don't know if you'll have the words, the delicacy, the strength. You think of the person on the other side: how you're about to bring their world crashing down with a single phone call and deep inside them they'll hate you because their sorrow will just be searching for someone to blame. Then what do you say? That you're sorry? Sorry for what? They'll hate you even more because they'll know you're not sorry like they are. They'll know you haven't been destroyed like they have.

Beeep. Beeep.

Maybe he wouldn't pick up, then I wouldn't have to speak to him. But what would I tell his father? The father with the crying eyes who knew it was time to give in to life, the one who just wanted a few last words, who wanted to say goodbye, who...

"Hello?"
"Good morning Sir, Dr Brown from Lancashire hospital speaking. I am calling regarding your father."
There was silence at the other end. I wondered what he had been doing. Had I called at the wrong moment? Was he already beginning to hate me? I thought he would never reply but he did – his voice appearing quite confident. I suspected he was holding back the tears.
"What about my father?" he said calmly.
"Your father is seriously ill," I took a deep breath. "He has asked to see you. He only has a few more hours."
Again, there was silence and this time I knew it had completely destroyed him. I empathised with his hatred towards me, despised myself and wished myself all the worst things in life because I knew he was thinking it too. After a long pause, the same calm voice surprised me. He was stronger than I was.
"Do you have a pen?" he said. Well, of course, I had a pen but why? I wasn't sure he understood.
"Yes, Sir, but I don't think you quite get me," I answered.
"Write down this number," he said softly, dictating me a number that sounded quite familiar. I knew I had heard it somewhere before.

"I've taken care of everything," he continued, "It's all been paid for, everything's been dealt with – took a while but I've done it. You won't have to worry about anything."
He didn't understand. I didn't understand. Who did he want me to call? A relative?
"It's the funeral service," he said before I could ask. "They'll take care of things. The coffin is ready – not just any coffin, mind you, it's a mahogany. That's the most expensive one."
I didn't know what to say.
"But your father... he asked to see you... he's not well. Your father is dying, Sir,"
"I'm a busy man," he replied, "I have to catch a plane to Tokyo in an hour. I'd like to come but I can't afford to miss that flight. Get him some flowers. Take the big bouquet."

I put the phone down with a trembling hand. Flowers? Would flowers be a good enough compensation? Flowers on a mahogany coffin. Perhaps we all die poor in the end. Maybe that's what we're worth – a coffin. I opened the door slowly, hoping he was asleep and would never know. He heard the door creak and turned his head, giving the biggest smile I had ever seen. It extended from ear to ear. There was light in his eyes, the kind of admiration in a father's eyes when he sees his son. What was I to tell him? That I was sorry? That his son had refused to come but sent him flowers and his regards? He didn't speak. I went up to his bed and kneeled down next to him. His smile would still not fade. I tried to think of the right words. I tried to find the strength.

Do you have a pen? Do you have a pen?

He would have the best coffin, the mahogany coffin, the one that had already been paid for. Who would come to the funeral? He would be alone with his flowers and his mahogany. Luxury without love.

Do you have a pen?

The waves seemed to tire. They moved slower, becoming flatter and flatter but still he smiled. *Beeep.* He had been younger before, he had watched people leave, he had been there but there was nobody there for him. *Beeeep.*

"My son," his voice came out as a hoarse whisper. "Are you here?" He held out a trembling hand to me. Nobody to take his hand.

"Son," he whispered again.

I grabbed the shaking hand and squeezed it tightly. Words no longer had any importance.

"Yes Dad," I said softly, "I'm here."

“Our biggest regrets are not for the things we have done but for the things we haven't done.”
Chad Michael Murray

8

Blue Box Story Number 8, April 2013

For the Cat

It was one morning in June, perhaps, when I first saw her, during one of those long summers where each day seemed the same. She wasn't a regular, no, but I'd seen her around for her face was not completely unknown to me. She was a small, fair lady who had undoubtedly been beautiful but whose face, now much older, looked more tired and wrinkled yet had a pleasant countenance. I remember my first thought being that I pitied her and quite honestly I did not know why for she was well-dressed and surely well-off. Still, there was something about her that stung my heart a little; maybe the fact that she was no longer as beautiful as she had once been or that she was no longer as young as she had once been. Maybe we all ought to feel sorry for ourselves because life is a tragedy and in the end we're all just little pieces stitched together desperately searching for something to hang on to. Perhaps all life is asking from us is a bit of attention. Maybe life just wants to be noticed, like a sulking toddler, so it will keep throwing things our way until we finally give it the attention it deserves.

I remember she wore a grey jacket which was peculiar for it was summer. Her hair was a variation of greys, well groomed but thinning in some places. I imagined she must have been a woman of high class with fancy clothes and expensive taste when she had been younger. Now, she clutched her handbag tightly with a sheepish smile and walked slowly, almost as if she knew not where to put herself.

"Good Morning!" My voice boomed with confidence. "What can I get you Ma'am? We've got meat fresh from this morning!" She looked away, as if embarrassed.

"Well this is going to sound silly," she said hesitantly. "It's just... my cat... well I was just wondering," Her voice sounded so small. "I'm sorry if this sounds rude but my cat you know... my cat likes meat very much and I was just wondering if you had any left-overs. Not anything for sale, oh no, just left-over pieces I could take home, if that's alright"

"Well of course!" I chuckled, "It's no trouble at all! In fact, I've got left-overs every day if you like."

At that she smiled and thanked me. I wrapped up a few left-over pieces of meat I had from the day. They weren't particularly good-looking or tasty, I imagined, but for a cat they would do just fine.

"And can I get you anything with that?" I asked.

"Er, well no," she looked embarrassed again, "er...not today, thank you."

"Alright then, Ma'am. Have a nice day!"

With that she had left, clutching her handbag and little paper bag of meat and I remember feeling sorry again as I watched her frail figure walk out the door.

Three days later she returned, with her same grey jacket, brown handbag and apologetic look. I had already prepared the meat. "Here you go Ma'am!" I smiled, "How did your cat like the meat? I hear cats enjoy those bits. Would you like anything else?" Again she thanked me and said that, no, this time she did not need anything else.

The days passed by. I watched them get shorter, I watched the skies with subtle variations of blue turn to night and the birds glide through them as if they owned everything underneath, flying in circles and feeling infinite because united they were strong. I watched the dappled leaves dance in the wind before falling slowly onto the concrete floor, dead yet beautiful, ending their lives with pride. I watched the clouds cry and the sky groan, like a sulking toddler refusing to settle down. Then I watched the bare trees that looked less majestic and imposing, maybe like us all in the end, as the streets wore their coat of white and the sky was no longer blue but grey. I observed the different outfits: the shirts, the sandals, the trousers and the jackets then eventually the thick coats and woollen scarves. I saw the faces change, the expressions differ. I watched life go on; the children grow, the babies walk, the adults hurry and with my big smile I greeted them all. Still she came. On Tuesday, Thursday and Saturday mornings she was there and she seemed more and more worn away and fragile, as though any moment she would break under the heaviness of the world. Yet still she came with her same handbag and grey jacket. She had started to become acquainted with another lady who was also a regular customer. I had got into the habit of collecting the left-overs of the day and putting them into a little bag for her. I had got into the habit of seeing her shy smile as her trembling hands clutched the paper bag. I had got into the habit of watching her eye the different meats before saying that no, she did not need any today. She had become a part of my little routine, of my life, if I can say. She had become one of those little things that made up my day just as we all feel comfortable with a routine because there is no unknown to fear when you know what to expect.

One Tuesday morning in January she did not come. I waited for her a little longer but still there was no sign of the little lady with the grey jacket. I told myself that perhaps she was busy that morning but couldn't help feeling a little worried. Thursday morning brought no sign of her either.

"Do you know where she could be?" I asked the other lady, "I've got the food for her cat but she doesn't seem to be coming." My voice came out smaller than I had anticipated. I realised I sounded ridiculous.

"Her cat?" the lady looked puzzled.
"Well yes," I explained, "I usually put the left-overs aside for the cat."
"But she doesn't have a cat..." the lady replied softly.
"Are you sure?"
"Yes. She's been living alone in her small room ever since her husband passed away. She had no children, it's sad, she has nobody."

When you're a child they tell you that you're safe. When you cry, they wipe up your tears and tell you that it's alright because everything always is alright in the end. The truth is that sadly, we all grow up living a lie but nobody wants to come out of it - why should we after all? We're so much more comfortable living in our ideal little bubble - thinking that bad things happen to bad people or just others but not to us, never to us because if we're nice the world should be nice back. Life is just like us. It wants to survive too and it wants to be noticed. Life wants all the attention. I don't know why it hurt me so much, maybe I felt blind. I felt as if I'd been blessed with eyes but hadn't seen. I hadn't seen the pain in her eyes or her smile. I hadn't realised that she had too much pride to come begging.

When she came back three days later, I saw

that her face was even more tired than usual. She seemed to have lost some hair. Her blood-shot eyes looked weak and sunken.
"Well Ma'am! Where you been?!" I said in my same cheerful voice. "I've been preparing the meat!"
"I'm sorry," she said softly, "I was a little unwell."
"Well that's alright," I smiled.
"No need to be sorry, here you go!"
I handed her the paper bag and she thanked me with her shy smile. Her lips were cracked.
"Hold on a second!" I said taking the bag back.
"I forgot something!" I took the bag to the back where she couldn't see and added two big pieces of the finest meat I had.
"Have a nice day!" I said.

She became a part of my routine again but not for long. I saw her state deteriorate every day. Sometimes, she would scare me. Her skin wrinkled and her smile disappeared. I continued to add some good meat. For the cat.

The days passed until one Tuesday morning again, when she did not come, and I felt a nagging constriction in my chest because I was afraid I would never see her shy smile and innocent eyes again. I didn't. They were no longer a part of my routine but perhaps now a part of my memory. I waited, though. I put the left-overs aside every day. At first, in their paper bag and then just to the side until finally I threw them away. The skies turned from a light blue to a darker blue. The leaves grew and fell and grew. The birds flew. The people rushed. Life threw fits. The wind blew. The clouds cried and the world kept spinning. I realised I didn't even have a name to associate to the image I had of the little lady in the grey jacket. She remained anonymous in my memory and sometimes, when I thought of her, I blushed out of shame or guilt although I knew it wasn't really my fault. Life isn't really our fault.

My hair turned from chestnut to light grey, the world spun and one summer morning in June as I emptied the bins I spotted a little grey kitten. The passers-by would have found me silly and, had I been a toddler or a child, I would have been told off by my mother but I went inside and got some meat. Two fine, expensive pieces. For the cat.

“What do you regard as most humane?
To spare someone shame.”
Friedrich Nietzsche

9

Blue Box story number 9, November 2013

Glowing Nights

When I was younger, I always thought the moon followed my car. I felt proud it had chosen mine and not any of the other cars. Whenever I rode in a car in the evening, I'd look out to see if the moon was following me and every time, there it was. There was some comfort in knowing something bigger and greater than myself was looking out for me. There was a warm feeling in seeing the mysterious silver ball lying in the sky like a great pearl and in telling myself that it was watching over me. When we passed tall buildings, I'd play peek-a-boo with the moon. It would hide behind a structure and I would count the seconds until it came back out again. Sometimes it took a while and I was afraid it had got lost or it didn't want to play with me anymore. After all, there was nothing special about me and there were other children who wanted to play with the moon. Suddenly, everything felt a little darker and my heart sank a little lower until, from behind a stretch of grey clouds, I'd catch a glimpse of silver and would smile because the moon was back for me again.

The moon didn't follow me when I was home. It hung still in its sky of dark clouds to watch over me and when I was alone or feeling afraid, I'd go over to my window and smile because the gentle moon would keep me company. The gentle moon would smile. One day I wondered if the moon would still follow me if I didn't have a car or if it would protect me if I didn't have a home. I wondered if it would be there when nothing else was, or if, like all other things, it left when times were hard. The thought had scared me and I had decided to look around when I was in my car and check if the people walking in the streets, who weren't in a home or in a car, also looked up as I did. It was then that I saw him for the first time.

He had eyes like those of a frightened animal;

they darted from side to side as car headlights reflected in them. He scurried between the cars waving glowing necklaces at the drivers with a pitiful look, before moving on as they shook their heads. He couldn't have been any older than I was and the thought of him being out there alone made me afraid. Where were his parents? I remember asking my own parents why such a little boy was out on the street by himself and why nobody seemed to want to buy the necklaces he was selling. Why didn't we buy one? Why didn't we help him? My question was answered by the traffic light turning green and the roar of nearby engines as everyone hurried to get to where they were going. I held my breath as the little boy zigzagged between the moving cars before safely reaching the pavement with his necklaces. He still had all of them. Nobody had bought anything.

Every time we passed by the Gulf Road, I asked the moon to let me watch the little boy instead. When the traffic light turned red, he only had a few minutes to try to sell his glowing necklaces. I observed as he waved them at car windows until someone handed him a note or some coins which he would tuck neatly into his pocket.

Whenever he came by our car, I would beg my mother to buy a necklace and lower my eyes so as not to make eye contact with him when I knew she didn't have change. I watched people turn their heads as he approached, pretending they could not see him even when he knocked at their windows or stuck his little face on the glass and smiled. Some pretended they were busy and others told him to go away. It hurt me to see people ignore him and my heart would stop for a moment when the traffic light turned green and he would have to sprint to safety. I wondered then why it was that some children had homes and cars and moons to protect them. I wondered why some could go to school and learn and hope to become greater people when others were condemned to living a life of begging, running and fear. I wondered why it was that I had been chosen to be one of the lucky children instead of him, when he was so much braver than I was.

The years passed and still I saw him. He grew. He was there almost every night with his necklaces that glowed against a moon greater than he was but who would not look after him. I stopped observing him because I could not do it without guilt in my heart and I became like all the others: those who looked but pretended not to see or those who simply turned their heads so there would be nothing to see at all.

As I got older, I stopped playing with the moon. I stopped paying attention to it or fantasising about its mysteries. There was nothing special about the moon. As things got more complicated, there was no more comfort or warmth in watching it. It followed me as it followed everyone else and when the clouds in the night sky were too dark, it hid behind them like the coward it was.

"Let us be grateful to the mirror for
revealing to us our appearance only."
Samuel Butler

10

Blue Box Story Number 10, December 2013

Thank You

In loving memory of Nada who flew away on a snowy afternoon.

I was always taught to say thank you. My mother said that when somebody did something for you, you had to thank them. She said letters were the best because people could keep letters. When you write something down, it stays forever. It's like a little part of you that you're giving to the universe and to that person too. So here is my thank you letter, the little part of me that I want you to have.

I want you to know that I was waiting. I know it's not nice to expect a gift - my mother says the best gifts are always a surprise. I love my mother but I disagree with her because I expected you every day and you were still the best present in the world. As much as I had tried to imagine you, when you came you were still a surprise.

The day you came it was cold and I was huddled in a corner with my little brother because he was cold too. We had been living in the basement for two weeks and I was thankful for the basement because it was protection, just like tears and screams; they are all protection. I did not know you were coming but, had I known, I would have been embarrassed; I would have tried to hide. I would have felt shameful with my emaciated figure, my little body that did not make me look like a man, and my bloodshot eyes. I would not have wanted to look at you because I was so ugly and pathetic, because we all were. And you would have looked at us children living in the dark and laughed because we were a sorry excuse for human beings. You would have laughed and laughed because you could not cry. Because sometimes you cannot cry.

Some days I would try to comb my hair with my fingers. I did that on the worst days; the days when I heard screaming and loud noises that chilled me to the bone. The days when there was no food and no love. The days when I could not hold my little brother and tell him things were alright because I did not want to lie. I would not be a liar. They are all liars. You are the only faithful one.

On those days in the basement, I would run my shaking hand through my hair so that it looked tidy. Then I would do the same for my brother so that he looked neat too and I would tell him to smile because you would be coming for us. So we would smile and sit in the dark and wait for you.

Some days I thought you had forgotten me or maybe you did not love me enough. I know it is not fair to expect love from someone who hardly knows you at all. I know that we are too young to understand and too old to understand and that perhaps nobody understands at all. I know that things happen for reasons we cannot comprehend and yet sometimes I really wish we could comprehend. I wish the world was not so dark. Sometimes it felt like somebody had turned off the lights and we were all suffocating in the darkness.

The day you did come, it was snowing and I imagined your dark figure enveloped in white. I imagined you were both cold and warm – that you bore both love and hate. When you came, you were disguised but I knew you straight away. You came as a man with a gun and I am sorry the children screamed. My brother cried too but I whispered to him that it was you and he squeezed my hand, tucked a strand of hair behind his ear and smiled.

Then you started. One by one you took us away. There were cries. The ground was black and red. When the man pointed the gun at my face, I smiled. I smiled because I saw you in his eyes and then there was sound and a light and my pathetic body fell to the floor. You wrapped yourself around me and enveloped me in your light and I was shivering but I was warm. You were every colour in the universe and I was a feather and together we went higher and higher and I could see everything from above. We soared into the sky and out of the darkness and I hated you but I loved you.

I don't understand why we hurt each other, perhaps I never will. In you I found relief and safety. In you I found happiness. So I say thank you - for me and on behalf of all the other children. Thank you for taking us away. Thank you for helping us escape and making us feel more free and alive than we ever have.

Here is the little part of me that will stay forever; the little part that will be yours. *Thank you for saving us.*

Emma Abdullah is a freelance writer and passionate debater. She has been writing for several magazines and hopes to be able to bring about change through her writing. At sixteen, this is her first book ever. Due to her mixed cultural background, Emma spends a lot of time travelling around the world and learning about different cultures. She hopes to go into politics and international law.

theblueboxstories@gmail.com